Keep Your Socks On, Albert!

by Linda Glaser

pictures by

Sally G. Ward

DUTTON CHILDREN'S BOOKS   NEW YORK

Library of Congress Cataloging-in-Publication Data

Glaser, Linda.
Keep your socks on, Albert!/by Linda Glaser;
illustrated by Sally G. Ward.
p.   cm.
Summary: Adventures of a young brother and sister who
enjoy each other but can't resist teasing.
ISBN 0-525-44838-1
[1. Brothers and sisters—Fiction.]   I. Ward, Sally G., ill.
II. Title.
PZ7.G48047Ke   1992
[E]—dc20   91-19387   CIP   AC

Published in the United States by Dutton Children's Books,
a division of Penguin Books USA Inc.
375 Hudson Street, New York, New York 10014

Printed in Hong Kong
First Edition 10 9 8 7 6 5 4 3 2

To my parents,
who inspire and encourage me
L.G.

To Lorraine
S.G.W.

Contents

Albert's Lost Sock

"I am sad," said Albert.

"One of my sailboat socks is missing.

I loved those socks!"

"Don't think about it,"

said Shirley.

"I will tell you a scary story.

It will take your mind off your sock.

Then you won't be sad."

"But I hate scary stories,"

said Albert.

"It has to be scary

if you want

to forget your sock,"

said Shirley.

"I will just stay sad,"

said Albert.

"No you won't,"

said Shirley.

"Albert, I want to help you.

So I won't make it too scary.

And just remember,

it's only a story."

8

Shirley's Scary Story

"Once there was a closet,"

Shirley began.

"That's not scary,"

said Albert.

"Not yet,"

said Shirley.

"Oh," said Albert.

Shirley went on.

"The closet was dark and creepy.

It was full of cobwebs.

And no one ever cleaned it

because it was shut tight."

"Is that the end of the story?"

asked Albert.

"Let's go out and play."

"Oh, no,"

said Shirley.

"An ugly zwibi lived in this closet.

It had sharp teeth.

It loved to eat cobwebs.

One day an opossum came by.

His name was Albert.

He heard a *scratch scratch*

from inside the closet door."

"I did not!"

said Albert.

"It wasn't *you*,"

said Shirley.

"This is only a story.

This opossum was afraid

of the noises.

He was afraid of *everything!*"

"I don't like this story,"

said Albert.

Shirley went on.

"More noises came from the closet.

They sounded like this.

Arggg. Snuffle. Arggg."

Albert covered his ears.

"I can't hear you," he said.

"ARGGG. SNUFFLE. ARGGG,"

yelled Shirley.

"I don't like this," said Albert.

"That is what Scared Albert

said in my story,"

said Shirley.

"Then his brave friend Shirley

came by."

"Are you in the story?"

asked Albert.

"Oh, no," said Shirley.

"I am much braver than

Brave Shirley in the story."

"You are not so brave, Shirley,"

said Albert.

"That is just what Scared Albert

said in my story,"

Shirley said.

"But he was wrong.

Brave Shirley went

right to the closet.

She knocked

on the door.

'Zwibi,

what do you want?'

she called.

'I want to get out,'

said the zwibi.

'I am hungry.

I have eaten

all the cobwebs.'

So Brave Shirley

reached for the doorknob.

Click . . .

Whoosh!

The zwibi rushed out.

It went right for Scared Albert.

It stuck its tongue out at him.

18

Zoom!

It ran away."

"Is that the end?"

asked Albert.

He came out from under the bed.

"Not quite,"

said Shirley.

"That zwibi

snuck right into

Scared Albert's closet!"

"It did?"

Albert whispered.

"Yes," said Shirley.

Then she smiled.

"But remember, it's only a story."

Albert gulped.

"Shirley, I need your help,"

he said.

"I need you

to clean my closet—

right away."

Closet Cleaning

Albert stood in front of his closet.

He was afraid to open the door.

"You have to clean

the zwibi out of my closet,"

he said.

"But that was only a story,"

said Shirley.

"I don't care," said Albert.

"Here's the broom."

Shirley opened the closet door.

CRASH! BUMP! THUMP! FLOP!

Out fell two pails,

two shovels,

one sock,

and two hats.

"Albert," said Shirley,

"this is a mess.

You should get rid of some stuff."

"Just the zwibi,"

said Albert.

Then he asked,

"Do you see it?"

Shirley stepped

into the closet.

"There is no zwibi,"

said Shirley.

"Good," said Albert.

"We're done."

"Oh, no," said Shirley.

"You need to get rid

of some of this junk."

Albert looked at all his things.

He put one pail,

one shovel,

and one hat in a pile.

"Get rid of this

sailboat sock too,"

said Shirley.

"You will never

find the lost one."

"Maybe I will," said Albert.

He took the sailboat sock.

Shirley looked at the pile on the floor.

"I will take this pile

away for you, Albert,"

she said.

"I will put it in *my* closet."

Eli the Monkey

Shirley opened her closet door.

It was very

neat inside.

"What is this?"

asked Albert.

"It's Eli, my monkey,"

said Shirley.

"He has a sore foot.

So he is wearing a bandage."

Albert frowned.

"This doesn't look like a bandage.

It looks like . . .

my lost sailboat sock!"

"Let me see,"

said Shirley.

She picked up the monkey

and held him close.

"Eli, did you take Albert's sock?"

asked Shirley.

She held Eli to her ear.

"Eli says he didn't take it,"

said Shirley.

"He found it somewhere."

"Shirley, that is my favorite sock.

Give it back!" said Albert.

"Bad Eli," said Shirley.

"He said it was a bandage."

Shirley untied the sock.

She handed it to Albert.

"Eli's foot is all better anyway,"

said Shirley.

"Now keep your socks on, Albert!

And help me find a place

for my pail

and shovel and hat."

"You can put them here,"

said Albert.

"No," said Shirley.

"Eli swings there."

"How about here?"

asked Albert.

"No," said Shirley.

"Eli sleeps there."

"I have an idea!"

said Albert.

"Let's go to the park.

We can take everything with us.

Then we won't have to

find a place to put anything."

Eli Gets Lost

Albert and Shirley

went to the park.

Shirley took Eli.

Albert wore his sailboat socks.

They headed right for

the sandbox.

Albert took off

his socks and shoes.

He jumped into the sand.

Shirley sat down.

"Let's make a cake," she said.

"No," said Albert.

"Let's make a mountain."

"I am going to make

a banana cake for Eli,"

said Shirley.

"You can make the mountain."

They both got to work.

"I'm done first!"

sang Shirley.

"Good," said Albert.

"Now you can help me."

They built

and patted

and smoothed.

Finally the mountain was done.

"Now Eli can climb it,"

said Shirley.

She looked around.

"Where is Eli?"

she asked.

"He was right next to you,"

said Albert.

"He's gone,"

said Shirley.

"He must be in the mountain."

"No!" said Albert.

"Yes! I'm sure,"

said Shirley.

"You are not!"

said Albert.

"Don't smash my mountain."

"It's *our* mountain,"

said Shirley.

"And *my* monkey is in it."

She smashed the mountain.

Eli wasn't there.

"I told you!"

cried Albert.

"Now you've ruined everything!"

"But where is Eli?"

asked Shirley.

She got up.

There was Eli.

Shirley had been sitting

on him.

"You're in trouble,"

Albert shouted.

"You broke my mountain!

And you squished Eli!"

Shirley hugged Eli.

"Eli isn't hurt," she said.

"He was hiding.

He thinks it's funny."

"Well, I don't,"

said Albert.

"We can make another mountain,"

said Shirley.

"Oh, all right," said Albert.

"But put Eli right here.

And keep him out of trouble."

"He says his feet are cold,"

said Shirley.

"He needs some socks."

"Not *my* socks!" said Albert.

He grabbed his socks

and stuffed them in his pail.

"You can keep your socks,"

said Shirley.

"I will tell Eli a scary story.

It will take his mind off his cold feet."

"No! It's my turn to tell,"

said Albert.

"But I will tell a *funny* story.

It is about a sneaky opossum.

Her name is Shirley."

"I don't like this,"

said Shirley.

"It's not about *you*,"

said Albert.

"And I won't make it *too* funny.

Just remember, Shirley,

it's only a story!"